THE SILVER MENACE

THE SILVER MENACE

MURRAY LEINSTER

WILDSIDE PRESS

Originally published as a two-part serial in *The Thrill Book*, Sept. 1, 1919 through Sept. 15, 1919.

Published by Wildside Press LLC.

www.wildsidebooks.com

CHAPTER I

The yacht was plowing through the calm waters with a steady throbbing of the engines. The soft washing of the waves along the sides, the murmur of the wind through the light rigging aloft, and the occasional light footstep of the navigating officer on the bridge were the only sounds.

The long white vessel swept on through the night in silence. Here and there a light showed from some port-hole or window, but for the most part the whole boat was dark and silent. For once the yacht contained no merry party of guests to one-step on the wide decks and fill all the obscurer corners with accurately paired couples.

Alexander Morrison, millionaire steamship magnate, and his daughter Nita had the ship to themselves. They were sitting in two of the big wicker chairs on the after deck, and the glow of Morrison's cigar was the only light.

"Getting chilly, Nita," he remarked casually. "Are you warm enough?"

"Yes, indeed." Nita was silent for a moment, gazing off into the darkness. "It's nice," she said reflectively, "to be by one's self for a while. I'm glad you didn't invite a lot of people to come back with us."

Her father smiled.

"Judging by the way you behaved along the Riviera," he reminded her, "you didn't mind company. I never saw any one quite so run after as you were."

Nita shook her head.

"They were running after you, daddy," she said lightly. "I was just a means of approach."

Her father puffed on his cigar for a moment in silence.

"It is a disadvantage, having a millionaire for a father," he admitted. "It's hard to tell who is in love with you, and who is in love with your father's money."

"So the thing to do, I suppose," said Nita amusedly, "is just to fall in love with some one yourself, and pay no attention to his motives."

"Where do you get your notions?" asked her father. "That's cynicism. You haven't been practicing on that theory, have you?"

"Not I," said Nita with a little silvery laugh. "But you know, daddy, it isn't nice to feel like a money bag with a lot of people looking at you all the time, some of them enviously and some of them covetously, but none of them regarding you just like a human being."

"I don't see," declared her father, with real affection, "how any normal young man who looked at you could stop thinking about you long enough to think about your money."

"I rise and bow," said Nita mischievously. "May I return the compliment, substituting 'young woman' for 'young man'?"

"Don't try to fool your father," that gentleman said with a smile. He added with something of conscious pride: "I don't suppose there are two other men in America as homely as I am."

"Daddy!" protested Nita, laughing. "You're lovely to look at! I wouldn't have you look a bit different for worlds."

"Neither would I have myself look different," her father admitted cheerfully. "I've gotten used to myself this way. I like to look at myself this way. It's an acquired taste like olives, but once you learn to like me this way—why, there you are."

Nita laughed and was silent. Suddenly she began to look a little bit puzzled.

"Do you notice anything funny?" she asked in a moment or so. "Somehow, the boat doesn't seem to be traveling just right."

Her father listened. Only the usual sounds came to his ears. The washing of the waves along the sides, however, had a peculiar timbre. Then he noticed that the boat seemed to be checking a little in its speed. There was an odd, velvety quality in the checking, very much like the soft breaking effect felt when a motor boat runs into a patch of weed.

"Queer," said Morrison. "We'll ask the captain."

The two of them walked down the deck arm in arm until they came to the stair ladder leading up to the bridge. The gentle checking continued. The boat seemed to be gradually slowing up, though the engines throbbed on as before.

"What's the matter, captain?" asked Morrison.

His first mate answered:

"I've sent for the captain, sir. Our speed has fallen off three knots in the past five minutes."

The captain came hastily up on the bridge, buttoning up his coat as he came.

"What's the matter, Mr. Harrison?"

The first mate turned a worried face to him.

"Our speed has dropped off three knots in five minutes, sir, and seems to be still slackening. I thought it best to send for you."

The captain called up the engine room.

"All right down there?"

"Per-rhaps," came the answer in a thick Scotch burr. "Ah was aboot to ask ye the same mysel'. We're usin' twenty perr cent more steam for the same number of rrevolutions."

"We might have run into a big patch of seaweed," suggested the first mate.

"Unship the searchlight," said the captain crisply.

A seaman came up to the bridge. He had been sent back to look at the patent log.

"We're logging eight knots now, sir."

The first mate uttered an exclamation.

"That's six knots off what we were making ten minutes ago!"

No one spoke for a moment or so, while one or two seamen worked at the lashing of the cover on the searchlight.

"Do any of you smell anything?" asked Nita suddenly.

A faint but distinct odor came to their nostrils. It was the odor of slime and mud, with a tinge of musk. It was the scent of foul things from the water. It was a damp and humid smell, indistinctly musklike and disgusting.

"Like deep-sea mud," said one of the seamen to the other. "Like somethin' come up from Gawd knows what soundin'."

Nita gasped a little. The searchlight sputtered and then a long, white pencil of light shot out over the water. It wavered, and sank to a point just beside the bow of the boat. It showed—nothing.

The bow wave rose reluctantly and traveled but a little distance before it subsided into level sea. There were no waves. The water was calm as an inland lake.

"No seaweed there," said the captain sharply. "Look on the other side."

The searchlight swept across the deck and to the water on the other side. Nothing. The water seemed to be turgidly white, but that was all. It was not clear; it was rather muddy and almost milklike, as if a little finely divided chalk had been stirred in it. There was no disturbance of its placid surface. Only the reluctant bow wave surged away from the sharp prow of the yacht.

The seaman returned from a second trip to the patent log.

"We're logging five knots now, sir."

"Nine knots off," said the first mate with a white face. "We were making fourteen."

"We'll take a look all around," said the captain sharply.

The searchlight obediently swept the surface of the water. Every one on the bridge followed its exploring beam with anxious eyes. That musky, musty smell of things from unthinkable depths and the mysterious retardation of their vessel filled them with apprehension.

There was not one of them, from the ignorant seamen to the supereducated Morrison, who did not look fearfully where the light beam went.

The hand laid on the vessel—that in a calm sea had slowed from fourteen knots to five, despite the mighty engines within the hull—that force seemed of such malignant power that none of them would have been greatly surprised to see the huge bulk of some fabled Kraken rearing itself above the water, preparing to engulf the yacht with a sweep of some colossal tentacle.

The sea was calm. As far as the searchlight could light up its surface not a wave broke its calm placidity.

The seaman returned from his third visit to the patent log. "Two knots, sir!"

The movement of the yacht became slower and slower as it gradually checked in its sweep through the water. The throbbing of the engines grew louder as they labored with increasing effort to master the mysterious Thing that was holding them back.

The boat was barely creeping now. It seemed to be struggling against some invisible force that gripped gently but relentlessly, some infinitely patient force that from the very patience of its operation was the more evidently inexorable.

The engines were working in panic-stricken tempo now. The chief engineer had given them all the steam they would take, and the propellers thrashed the water mightily, but the ship slowed, slowed.

At last it was still, while the engines seemed to be trying to rack themselves to pieces in their terrific attempt to drive the ship against the Thing that held it back.

The captain watched with a set face, then ordered the engines reversed. There was an instant's pause, and the propellers took up their thrashing of the water again. For a moment it seemed that they would have some effect. The yacht shivered and moved slightly backward, but then stopped again with the same soft gentleness.

The seamen inspected the water all around the ship with lanterns lowered to the water's edge. They found nothing. A sounding line was thrown overboard, and sank for two hundred fathoms without reaching bottom.

The searchlight played endlessly over the water, trying to find some turmoil that might indicate the presence of a monster whose tentacles had fastened upon the ship, but without result. The surface of the water was like glass.

Again and again the engines struggled mightily to move the ship. Again and again the propellers beat the water at the stern into froth and foam, but never did the yacht move by as much as an inch.

The sea was calm and placid. The stars looked down from the moonless sky and were reflected by the still surface of the water.

The yacht struggled like a living thing to break free from the mysterious force that held her fast, while all about her there hung that faintly disgusting odor of slime from the depths of the sea, an indistinctly musky odor as of something unclean.

At last the wireless began to crackle a frantic appeal for help, giving the details of what was happening on board the yacht. Hardly had the message finished when the yacht began to rock slightly, as from a faint ground swell.

CHAPTER II

"But, Theodore, old pet," said Davis amiably. "The fact that a plane won't loop the loop or make nose dives at ninety degrees doesn't make it hopeless as a battleplane."

He was affectionately expounding the good points of a monster seaplane drawn up in its hangar by the beach.

Davis wore the insignia of a flight commander of the aviation corps and the ribbons of half a dozen orders bestowed on him after the destruction of the Black Flyer, destroyed by Teddy Gerrod and himself some six months before.

Teddy Gerrod was in civilian clothes, but was earnestly, though cheerfully, disputing everything his friend said.

"A two-seater like the one we used six months ago," he pointed out, "could fly rings around this bus of yours, and with a decent shot at the machine gun could smash it in no time."

"Fly rings around it? Not noticeably," said Davis confidently. "Since our idea of platinum plating the cylinders everybody's doing it. Using picro gasoline, as you and I did, we get a hundred and eighty miles an hour from this 'bus' you're trying to disparage. And, furthermore, if you try to damage this particular ship with machine-gun bullets you're going to be disappointed."

"Armor?"

"Precisely. I admit cheerfully that you may know a lot about physics and cold bombs and liquid gases and such things, but when it comes to flying machines—my dear chap, you simply aren't there."

Gerrod laughed.

"Perhaps not. But I'd rather dance around in a more lively fashion in a little two-seater."

"And privately," admitted Davis, "so would I. The next war we have I'm going to arrange for you to be my machine gunner."

"Delighted," said Gerrod. "But what would Evelyn say?"

He was referring to his wife. Davis waved his hand.

"Oh, she'd say there aren't going to be any more wars."

"That reminds me," said Gerrod. "We want you down for the next weekend. No other guests."

Davis nodded abstractedly. A messenger was coming over to the hangar at double time.

"Thanks. I'll be glad to come. Wonder what this chap wants?"

The messenger came up, saluted, and handed Davis a yellow slip. Davis tore it open and read:

Steam yacht *Marisposita*, Alexander Morrison of New York, owner, reports position 33°11'N 55°10'W, wants immediate assistance. Engines and hull perfect condition, not aground, no derelict or obstacle discoverable. Unable to move any direction. Sea calm. Only possible explanation has been seized by sea monster. Flt. Comm. Richard Davis ordered to make reconnaissance of situation in seaplane. Reported condition considered incredible, but no naval vessels in immediate vicinity. Flt. Comm. Richard Davis will make immediate investigation and report.

Davis whistled.

"Here's something pretty!" he remarked. "Take a look."

He handed the order to Gerrod and went quickly to the door leading into the workshop attached to the hangar.

In a few crisp sentences he had ordered the big plane prepared for an extended flight, with provisions and as much fuel as it would carry. He returned to find Gerrod thinking busily.

"May I come along on this trip?"

"It's against regulations, of course," said Davis, "but no one will kick if *you* go. You're privileged."

He cried an order or so at the workmen, who were now swarming over the machine.

Although the wireless message had been sent from the yacht after nightfall, the sun was barely setting on the coast, where the hangar was placed.

The vessel in distress was some thirty degrees east of the coast, and consequently the sun set two hours before it sank on the coastal line.

Gerrod phoned a hasty message to his wife and went to Davis' quarters, where he borrowed heavy flying clothes from Davis' wardrobe. The mechanics and helpers worked with desperate haste.

The aëroplane would be flying all night long, but it was desirable that it take off while there was yet some light. The long fuel tank was filled, and the motors run some ten or fifteen minutes, while critical ears listened for the faintest irregularity in their bellowing roar.

Two engineers and a junior pilot were to go with Davis in the big aircraft, and they were hastily summoned and told to prepare to leave in as short a time as possible.

It was hardly more than half an hour from the time the telegraphed order was received before Gerrod preceded Davis up the ladder and into the inclosed cabin of the seaplane.

The motors were cranked—two men tugging at the blade of each of the huge propellers—and the plane slid slowly down the ways and into the water.

Davis maneuvered carefully until he was clear of all possible entanglements. Then he gave the motors more gas and more. Their harsh bellow rose to a deafening sound, and the long, boatlike body began to surge through the waves with gradually increasing speed.

For a few yards the spray blew upon and spattered the glass windows of the cabin. Then the planes began to exert their lifting power and the plane began to ride the waves instead of plowing through them.

The speed increased again, and suddenly the shocks of the waves beating on its under surface ceased. The plane rode upon air with a smooth and velvety motion that was sure and firm.

Davis rose gradually to five thousand feet and headed accurately to the east. A southerly wind, reported by wireless from a ship at sea, would carry him slightly to the south, and the sum of the two motions should bring him, by dawn, very close to the spot from which the yacht had sent out her wireless call.

Davis was not pushing the plane to its utmost. He would need light by which to descend, and had no intention of reaching the spot where the *Marisposita* was in distress until dawn.

From their altitude the ocean seemed only a dark, unfathomable mass below them. The stars twinkled down from the arch of the sky in all their myriads of sizes and tints.

There was no moon. Those in the closed car of the big seaplane could only see the star-strewn firmament above them and upon all sides, which sank down, and abruptly was not.

Save for the cessation of the star clusters, the horizon was invisible. The sea was obscure and mysterious, like some mighty chasm over which they flew precariously.

The dark wings of the plane stretched out from the sides of the body with a mighty sweep. The plane was over a hundred feet across, and with the powerful motors it possessed was capable of lifting an immense weight. Even now more than two tons of fuel were contained in the huge tanks in the tail.

Davis drove steadily on through the night for a long time. His face was intent and keen. He made little or no attempt to look out of the windows before him.

His eyes were fixed almost continuously upon the instruments before him: the altometer, which was a barometer graduated to read in feet and with means for correcting the indication by barometric readings from sea level; the inclinometer, which showed the angle at which the plane was traveling with regard to the earth's surface, and the compass.

The compass was one of the very latest developments of the gyroscopic compass and showed the true north without regard for magnetic deviations.

Davis felt out his machine thoroughly and then turned it over to his junior pilot. The younger man—and to be younger than Davis meant that he was very young indeed—slipped into the driver's seat, quickly ascertained the course, speed, and altitude, and settled back to continue Davis' task, while Davis curled himself up in a chair and went instantly to sleep.

It was chilly in the car, but Davis slept the sleep of the just, ignoring the roaring of the motors outside, which was only slightly muffled by the windows of the car.

Gerrod had gone to sleep some time before, and one of the two engineers was similarly curled up on the floor of the roomy and comfortable car.

Hours passed, while the big seaplane winged its way steadily through the night. It roared its way across the vast chasm of the dark ocean below, an incarnation of energy at which the placid stars looked down in mild surprise.

The exhausts roared continuously, the stays hummed musically, and the great wings cut through the air with resistless force.

Within the dark body of the plane three men slept peacefully, one sat up sleepily, listening to the motors, and prepared to wake into alertness at the slightest sign of irregularity in the action of any of them, and one man sat quietly at the controls, his eyes fixed on the instruments before him, lighted by tiny, hooded electric bulbs.

Course, due east. Altitude, five thousand feet. Speed, one hundred and fifteen miles. Twice during the night Davis woke and made sure that all was well.

In leaving the navigation of the machine to his assistant, he was not throwing the major part of the work on him. The work would come in the morning, when they found the yacht.

If there were anything in the talk of a sea monster having seized the yacht, Davis would need to be fresh for the search and possible battle that would follow.

He was taking the most sensible precaution possible. And, in any event, he had driven for the first four hours, during which the younger man had rested.

The first gray light began to appear in the east. The pilot of the plane had not looked away from his instruments for an hour, and not until a faint light outside called his attention to the approach of dawn did he think to glance through the windows.

A dimly white glow was showing as an irregular splotch toward the east. The pilot saw it and noticed something odd about its appearance, but did not stop to examine it closely.

He called Davis, as he had been ordered to do. Davis sat up, rubbed his eyes, and was thoroughly awake.

"All right?" he asked.

The pilot nodded.

"Sunrise," he said. "You said to call you."

"Right you are." Davis stood up and stretched his muscles. "Here, Teddy, wake up."

Gerrod stirred, and in a moment was awake. Davis deftly prepared coffee and sandwiches.

"Rescuers like ourselves need to be fed," he observed with a smile. "I wonder what is actually the matter with that person Morrison?"

"Millionaires are timid folk," Gerrod agreed. "I'll bet we've had a wild-goose chase."

"Funny, though," said Davis ruminatively. "People don't usually send out wild wireless messages like that. They probably ran into a big bunch of seaweed."

He bit into a sandwich. The two engineers, with complete democracy, were already eating. The man at the controls suddenly uttered an exclamation.

"What's the matter?" asked Davis quickly.

"Look out the window," said the pilot in a tone indicating that he could not believe his eyes.

Davis looked, and his month dropped partly open. Before them the white patch of light had turned golden and then yellow. A bank of clouds lay before them, behind which the sun was evidently hidden.

That had not caused Davis' exclamation, however. He was not amazed at anything he saw, but at the lack of something he did not see—the ocean. The cloud bank was illuminated by the sun. It covered half of the sky before them, *and below them*!

There was no ocean below them. There was no land below them. Above, the rapidly graying sky could be seen. Below them was rapidly graving sky! There was no horizon, there was no land, there was no sea.

There was only sky. They seemed to be alone in an illimitable firmament, a derelict in open space, adrift in some unthinkable ether in which there was no landing space or any solid thing except themselves.

Above them and below them, before them and behind them, on their right side and their left side was sky, and nothing but sky. There was not one bit of solid matter visible on either side, ahead or behind, up or down.

It was as if they had gone aloft, and while they flew the earth had been destroyed. Only the incredibility of such a catastrophe kept them from believing it instantly.

"Teddy," said Davis in a moment or two, trying to jest, though his voice was shaking, "you're our tame scientist. What's happened to our well-beloved earth? Has it gone off and left us in the lurch? Have we flown off into space?"

Gerrod was looking with all his eyes. He looked down into a blue bowl that was the exact counterpart of the dome above.

"Which way is down?" he asked quietly. "Is it that way, or that way?" He pointed over his head and at his feet. "Are we flying right side up, or upside down, or what?"

The plane banked sharply and side-slipped for a moment before it recovered.

"Steady!" said Davis to the man at the controls. "Steady—"

The machine banked again, then shot upward, stalled, and slipped on again.

"Straighten out!" said Davis sharply. "Up with the joy stick!"

"I don't know what's what," said the white-faced pilot desperately, obeying as he spoke. "Great God! What's happening now?"

The plane seemed to be standing on its tail, and the three men standing in the car slid toward the rear. Davis seized a seat and clambered toward the controls. As he made his way toward the instruments the plane seemed to go mad.

It twisted, turned, stood upon its head and darted forward, and then seemed to be wallowing in the air. Davis seized the controls, and with his eye solely on the inclinometer worked madly for a moment. The plane stopped its antics and drove on steadily.

"It's like driving in a fog," he said over his shoulder. "All right back there now?"

"Yes." Gerrod was answering. "What happened?"

"With nothing to tell which was up and which down, we lost our level and couldn't find it again. I've flown upside down for five minutes, going through a cloud, and didn't know it until my barometer dropped upward. We're all right, but what's happened to the earth?"

Gerrod cautiously made his way to a point beside Davis, who was driving with his eyes glued to the instruments. That incredible vastness into which the machine seemed to be boring was appalling. They seemed to be speeding madly from nothingness into nothingness, with nothing below them and nothing above.

They were alone in a universe of air. Gerrod stared ahead at the cloud bank behind which the sun seemed to be hiding.

"There's the sun, all right. What's our barometer reading?"

"Eight thousand feet."

"Try dipping, by the inclinometer."

Davis did so. Though there was not the slightest change in the appearance of the sky that compassed them all about, the barometer quivered from eight thousand feet to seven, and then to six. Gerrod suddenly uttered an exclamation:

"The sun's coming out!"

The fiery disk of the sun peered slowly from behind the edge of the cloud bank.

"There's *another*!"

From the opposite side of the cloud bank a second sun could be seen, slowly appearing as had the first. The two suns swam away from the fringe of the cloud and glared at each other.

"I've got it!" Gerrod struck his knee with his hand. "What fools we are!"

"I'm glad we're only fools," said Davis mildly. "I've been afraid we had gone mad. What's happened?"

"Why, the water," Gerrod said excitedly, "the water is perfectly calm and reflects like a mirror. We don't see the sky below us. We see the reflection of the sky. And that isn't a second sun," he pointed; "that's the reflection of the sun."

"Only, the water doesn't reflect like that," said Davis. "At least, not from straight overhead. Open a side window and look directly downward."

Gerrod did so, and exclaimed again:

"I'm right, I tell you! Directly under us I can see the reflection of our plane, flying upside down."

Davis took a quick glance.

"I guess you are right, after all," he admitted, "but the water doesn't reflect like that normally. Something queer must have happened." He was silent a moment, while his eyes swept the distance before them keenly. "Here's another proof you're right. There's the yacht we're looking for."

Far away, its white hull turned to red gold by the first rays of the sun, they saw the yacht, motionless on the water. And in striking corroboration of Gerrod's hypothesis, they saw every line and every spar reflected in the water below.

Davis shifted his course to bear for the yacht and dipped down until he was only five hundred feet above the strange, mirrorlike surface of the sea. Below them they could see the spreading wings of their seaplane reflected from the still water.

They swept up to the yacht and circled above it. The junior pilot unshipped the tiny wireless set of the aëroplane, and it crackled busily for a few moments.

"All right to alight," he reported. "They say nothing has happened all night, but they're still unable to move."

The plane swept around the yacht in a wide circle, coming lower and lower. It was quite impossible to judge where the surface of the water might be, but Davis kept his eye on the deck of the yacht, to get the level from that.

At last he made his decision. Being quite unable to tell exactly where the surface was, he could not land in the usual fashion. He slowed in mid-air until the machine was moving at the lowest speed at which it would keep aloft.

Then, by a jerk of the joy stick, he headed it upward at an angle it was unable to make at that speed. The result was that the machine stalled precisely like a motor car on an upgrade and, with next to no headway, "pancaked," sank vertically—downward.

"Sit tight!" he ordered as the plane sank.

Next moment every one of them clutched wildly at the nearest object to keep himself from falling. The plane had struck the surface, but instead of skimming forward, as its slight remaining headway made it try to do, it was brought to a sudden standstill as if by a mighty brake.

Only a miracle kept it from overturning. Davis opened a window of the cabin and shouted:

"Throw us a rope and haul us alongside!"

The men on the deck of the yacht heard him, and a rope came hurtling through the air, to fall across one of the wings.

Davis scrambled out and made it fast. Those on the yacht hauled, but the plane did not move. Half a dozen men grasped the slender line and threw their united weight upon it. The rope broke with a snap.

"What the—" exclaimed Davis in astonishment.

A second rope was thrown. The captain of the yacht called from the bridge:

"Haul a heavy line to you and make that fast!"

Wondering, those on the seaplane obeyed. The sailors on the yacht made the other end of the stouter line fast to a capstan and manned it. Slowly and reluctantly the seaplane was drawn toward the white vessel.

It was Gerrod who looked behind them. Where the float of the seaplane had been he saw a deep depression in the surface of the water, which, as he watched, slowly filled.

"The sea is turned to jelly!" he exclaimed, and he was right.

They found the truth of the matter when they clambered on board the yacht. With the morning, the members of the crew were able to make a more thorough investigation of what had happened.

They lowered boats, and the boats stuck fast. When oars were dipped into the strangely whitened or silvered water the oars were drawn out coated with a sticky, silvery mass of a jellylike substance.

From the deck of the yacht the altered appearance of the sea was as remarkable as from the air. All of the ocean seemed to have been changed to a semisolid mass of silver.

The horizon had vanished or ended into the sky imperceptibly so it could not be distinguished. The captain discussed the matter with them.

"I've never seen anything like this before," he said perplexedly. "I've been on a ship that traveled two hundred miles on a milk sea, but never anything like this."

"What do you think it is?" asked Davis. "Something on the order of a milk sea?"

The captain nodded.

"You know a milk sea is caused by a multitude of little animals that color the water milky white. They're phosphorescent at night. This must be something on that order, only these cluster together until the water is made into a jelly. And they have a queer, slimy smell."

"They aren't phosphorescent," said Davis.

"No, of course not."

Nita Morrison had joined the little group. Her father was beside her, looking rather worried.

"Well," said Nita anxiously, "what's to be done? How are we going to get the yacht free?"

"I'm afraid we aren't," said Davis, smiling. "The telegraphed orders that brought me here told me simply to make an examination and make a report. My plane can't do anything for the yacht, of course."

"Then what—"

"I'll go back and report," Davis explained, "and they'll send boats to try to get in to you people. There doesn't seem to be any immediate danger, and at worst you can all be taken off by aëroplane, if we can rise again from that jelly mess."

Nita wrinkled her small nose.

"I know we aren't in danger," she said, "or at least I know it now, but are we going to have to stay here and smell that horrid smell until the government gets ready to rescue us?"

The odor of the jellylike animalcules was far from pleasant. It was an unclean scent, as of slime dredged from the bottom of the sea.

"Well-l," said Davis thoughtfully, "I dare say we can accommodate two more people. It isn't quite regular, but that's a detail."

"But the crew?" Morrison looked inquiringly at the captain of the yacht.

"Milk seas always break up, sir," said the captain. "I have no doubt this silver sea will break up as well. We can wait and see, and at worst we have our wireless."

"Then it's settled," said Nita joyfully. From sheer gratitude she smiled at Davis.

"Always providing we can get aloft again," said Davis.

"The propellers of the ship, sir," suggested the captain, "though they can't move the yacht, yet manage to thrash a fair-sized patch of this jelly into liquid."

"A good idea," said Davis heartily. "We'll haul the plane around to the stern, and you'll set your engines running."

In a very little time this was done. The great propellers of the yacht thrashed mightily, and a narrow patch of open water opened in the silver sea. The seaplane was laboriously hauled around to the stern of the yacht, and the party was lowered on board.

With some difficulty the motors were cranked again and the plane scuttled madly down the lane of water. With a quick jerk of the joy stick Davis lifted the plane from the water just as the open water ended and the silver sea began.

The big plane circled in the air, rising steadily as it circled, and at last headed for the west again, still flying in that incredible appearance of sky above and sky below, with the reflected sun glaring upward just as fiercely as the real sun beat down.

CHAPTER III

Nita sat in the seat beside Davis' control chair, pointing to the instruments one by one.

"And that's the inclinometer," she repeated, "to tell you the angle at which the plane is climbing or descending. That's the barometer, which reads—let me see—seventy-four hundred feet. We're over a mile high, aren't we?"

"We are," said Davis, "though by the looks of things we are ten thousand miles from anywhere."

The silver sea was still beneath them, and they still seemed to be floating in a universe of air. Nita paid no attention.

"And that's the compass dial, and that—What did you call it?"

"An anenometer," said Davis again, smiling. "It's the speedometer of the air—or the patent log, whichever you like to call it."

"You only have to learn one syllable," said Nita. "They all end in ometer. It's convenient that they're named like that."

Davis smiled.

"I never thought of that before, but it is convenient."

"But how do you balance the plane?" Nita demanded.

"In straightaway flight it balances itself," Davis explained. "It's one of the new inherently stable designs. For turning, the wing tips work automatically. We've a gyroscopic affair that attends to them."

Nita subsided for a moment, then demanded further information.

"What's that lever for? To change speeds?"

Davis laughed.

"Well, no. We haven't but one speed forward and no reverse—"

"You're making fun of me!"

"That's the joy stick," said Davis, chuckling. "We dive and climb with it. Pull it back and we go up. Push it forward and we dive."

"Mmmmm," said Nita interestedly.

Her father took his cigar out of his mouth long enough to join in Davis' chuckle at Nita's absorbed air.

"Don't talk to the motorman, Nita," he said. "He may run past a switch."

Nita turned around and smiled at him. The car was rather crowded with seven people in it. Gerrod was looking curiously at a bit of the silvery jelly, with which he had filled several pails before leaving the yacht. He took a bit of it between his thumb and forefinger and rolled it back and forth speculatively.

It seemed faintly granular to the touch, but at the slightest pressure underwent a change that felt like crumbling, and was nothing but watery liquid.

"I'll bet anything you care to name," he said thoughtfully, "that this is just a mass of little animalcules with little silvery shells. The silvery shells would account for the reflection we see."

"The captain of my yacht," observed Morrison, "said that he thought it was like a milk sea. That's a mass of little animals that glow like phosphorus in the dark."

"Perhaps," said Gerrod meditatively. "I'd like to look at this stuff under a microscope."

"Oh some of it will go to the government chemists," said Morrison with a large air, "and they'll figure out a way to kill the little beasts. There's a cure for everything."

"Perhaps," said Gerrod.

The plane flew on steadily, Davis finding some amusement in gratifying Nita's suddenly aroused curiosity about every part of the seaplane. When her curiosity about the plane was satisfied, however, and she began to make inquiries about himself, Davis was much less comfortable.

He tried to be evasive, but she pinned him down, and was filled with excitement when she found that he was the same man who, as Lieutenant Davis, had flown the two-seated flying machine that had destroyed the Black Flyer and with it Varrhus' menace to the liberty of the world.

She tried very hard indeed to get him to tell her the story of that fight, but he blushed and said there was nothing to tell. It would be hard to say to what lengths she would have gone had not something outside the plane caught her attention.

"There's the horizon!" she exclaimed. "We've come to the edge of the silver sea, and from here on it's just the plain, good, old-fashioned ocean."

The line that marked the point where sea and sky joined was indeed visible, and a gradually widening bank of darker blue showed that the silver sea had indeed come to an end.

As the seaplane flew onward the darker, wave-tossed ocean came toward them and passed below, but blended so gradually with the jellied ocean that it was impossible to tell where the silver sea ended and blue water began. It was evident that the silver sea was still growing.

Then, for a long time, the seaplane sped onward over the blue waters, while Nita tried ingeniously to extract from Davis the details of the fight with the Black Flyer.

Davis was acutely uncomfortable, but nevertheless he felt strangely disappointed when the dim line of the coast appeared ahead. He hovered a moment to get his bearings, and then sped northward toward the aviation station to which he was attached.

Nita, too, seemed disappointed. She had enjoyed tormenting Davis, and he impressed her very favorably. After the plane had swooped downward and come to rest on the water a scant two hundred yards from the hangar in which it was kept, she turned to Davis.

"Well," she announced, "since I haven't been able to make you tell me what I want to know this time I warn you I shall make you tell me next time."

Davis smiled.

"May I hope there will be a next time?"

Nita smiled at him.

"I shall be angry if there isn't," she said demurely.

The launch came up to tow them ashore, and Davis was busy for a few moments, but before Nita and her father climbed into the motor car they had commandeered to take them to the city he found time to make a more definite arrangement and learned he was expected to call at the Morrison mansion "very, very soon."

The description of the silver sea aroused but little attention in the newspapers. A particularly pathetic murder trial was filling the public mind, and small paragraphs in obscure corners, describing the plight of the yacht, contained all that the public learned.

Every one seemed to dismiss the matter as a natural curiosity which would probably disappear in a little while. An aggregation of tiny animalcules which had clustered together until they formed a jellylike mass did not promise much in the way of drama, and our newspapers are essentially purveyors of drama.

Obscure notices in the shipping news, however, told of the growth of the silvery patch, and at last there was a ripple of interest caused by the news that the crew of the yacht claimed that the jellylike creatures were clambering up the sides of the ship and threatening to overwhelm the vessel.

Seaplanes put out from shore and took the crew off, and then public interest lapsed again. An almost uneventful accident to the yacht of a steamship magnate was good material for society news, but not for the pages devoted to items of general interest.

To Davis, however, anything pertaining to Nita had become of surpassing interest. He practically haunted her house, and Nita seemed not at all unwilling to have him there. Her father was as cordial as Nita at first, but later began to watch Davis' frequent appearances with something of disquiet.

Davis was sufficiently well known from his Black Flyer episode to be considered socially eligible anywhere, but he was far from rich. He had consistently refused the numerous offers from motion-picture companies and book publishers to enact or relate his exploits, though the acceptance of any of those offers would have meant a small fortune.

Davis was instinctively unwilling to commercialize his reputation. Morrison could find no fault with him personally, but he could not quite believe that Davis' increasingly evident infatuation for Nita was real—that he was actually more than a fortune hunter.

The shipping news continued to give sparsely phrased notice of the location and size of the silver sea. Two naval vessels were assigned to observe it, reporting regularly to the meteorological bureau.

It must be recorded to the credit of that much-maligned department of weather forecasts and maritime information that it was probably the first body to see the possibilities of evil that lay in the silver sea.

It had quantities of the silvery mass of animalcules brought to it for study, and set its scientists to work to try and find a means of destroying them. Fish would not eat them. They seemed to possess some repulsive taste that led all the carnivorous fishes to avoid them at all costs. Placed in an aquarium with a huge sea bass that was exceptional for its voracity, the sea bass avoided the tiny, jellylike mass as it would the plague.

The silver globule of jelly multiplied in size, and still the sea bass avoided it, retreating to the farthest corners of its tank to keep from coming in contact with the little animalcules. At last the aquarium was a shimmering mass of silvery, sticky jelly, and the bass was unable to retreat farther. It was found gasping out its life outside the tank, having leaped from the water to escape from the omnipresent silver menace.

The silver sea grew in size. It began to figure in the news again, when passengers on the transatlantic liners noticed that the steamers were taking a route much farther to the north than was customary. It was admitted at the steamship offices that the detour was made for the purpose of avoiding, the now vast silver sea.

Late in March people along the eastern coast of the United States began to remark upon a musklike, slimy smell that was faintly discernible in the sea breeze. A steamer, going from New York to Bermuda, reported seeing a patch of the silvery jelly only three hundred miles from the eastern coast. The disagreeable, musklike smell was strong and noticeable.

The newspapers woke to the possibilities of the silver sea. Ships could not navigate in its jellied waters, nor fish swim. It covered thousands of square miles now, and was growing with an ominous steadiness that foreboded ill.

The seaside resorts along the Atlantic coast were practically abandoned. Tourists would not stay where that foul, slimy, musklike scent was borne to them constantly on the sea breeze. The patches that were the forerunners of the silver sea itself appeared along the coast. At last the horizon disappeared.

The silver sea had come close, indeed, to the shore. Then every newspaper burst into huge headlines. For the different papers they were phrased differently, but the burden of each, displayed in the largest possible type, was

COASTAL NAVIGATION STOPPED!

America's Communication With the World Cut Off By Silver Sea.—Harbor Blocked from Maine to Georgia.—Authorities Helpless to Fight Silver Menace.

Then the world began to be afraid.

CHAPTER IV

Davis was unwontedly silent as Gerrod drove him out to the tiny cottage to which he had been invited.

"Evelyn's expecting you," said Gerrod as the little motor car wound up a hill between banks of fragrant trees that line the road on either side. "We rather looked for you last week, but you wired, you know."

"Yes, I know," said Davis gloomily. "I went somewhere else."

Gerrod smiled. Davis was sufficiently his friend to break an engagement and admit it frankly, and besides Gerrod more than suspected where Davis had gone.

"How is Miss Morrison?" he asked.

"She's all right," said Davis still more gloomily. "But damn her father!"

Gerrod raised his eyebrows and said nothing until they arrived at the cottage with the little built-on laboratory. Evelyn came out at the sound of the motor and shook hands with Davis.

"We were beginning to be afraid the competition was too much for us," she said with a smile.

Davis looked at her and tried to smile in return, but the result was a dismal failure.

"Oh, I'm glad to be here now," he said dolefully.

Gerrod made a sign to Evelyn not to refer to Nita again until he could speak to her, and helped Davis carry his two suit cases into the house.

"Your usual room, of course," he said cheerfully. "Dinner is served at the same hour as before, and you can do just as you please until you feel like coming down. I'll be in the laboratory."

Davis went heavily upstairs, his usually cheerful face suffused with gloom. Evelyn glanced at Gerrod.

"What's the matter?" she asked quickly. "Has he quarreled with Nita?"

Gerrod shook his head, smiling.

"I asked about her, and he answered by damning her father. I suspect he has run against a little paternal opposition."

Evelyn's eyes twinkled and she laughed.

"Best thing in the world for them," she declared. "When he's ripe for it I'll take a hand. Nita Morrison was a classmate of mine in college and I know her well enough to help along."

Gerrod chuckled.

"He was like a funeral all the way out. We'll let him alone until he wants to talk, and then you can advise him all you like. But just now I want to get back at those small animals that are raising so much particular Cain."

He went into the laboratory and slipped off his coat. He had a number of test tubes full of the silvery animalcules and was examining them under all sorts of test conditions to determine their rate of growth and multiplication.

He was rather hopeful that he would be able to demonstrate that after a certain period they would—because of their extremely close packing together—either die from inability to obtain nourishment or be poisoned from their own secretions.

He was looking curiously at a phenomenon that always puzzled him when Davis came into the room. His expression was that of a man utterly without hope.

"What've you got there?" he asked listlessly.

"Some of our silvery little pets," said Gerrod cheerfully. "I'm studying them in their native lair. Have you looked at them under a microscope?"

"No."

Gerrod smeared a bit of the silvery mess on a glass slide and put it under a microscope. He worked busily for a moment or so, adjusting the focus, and then waved Davis toward the eyepiece.

"They're funny little beasts. Look them over."

Davis looked uninterestedly, but in a moment even his gloom was lightened by the interest of the sight he saw. The enlargement of the microscope was so great that only a few of the tiny animals were visible, but each of them was clearly and brilliantly outlined.

They were little jellylike creatures, roughly spherical in shape, with their bodies protected by almost infinitely thin, silicious shells that possessed a silvery luster. From dozens of holes in the fragile shells protruded fat, jellylike tentacles that waved and moved restlessly, forever in search of food.

Under the microscope the shells were partly transparent, and within the jellylike body inside the shell could be seen a single dark spot.

"That blotch in their shells seems to be the nucleus, or else their stomach. I can't quite make out if they're one-celled animals like am[oe]bæ, or if they're really complex creatures."

"Rum little beggars," said Davis without removing his gaze from the eyepiece. "They're separate animals, anyway. Odd that they should make a jellylike mass."

"Move the slide about a little," suggested Gerrod. "You'll see how they do that. You're looking at individuals now. Sometimes—and I think it's when food gets scarce—they twine their tentacles together and the tentacles actually seem to join, as if they were welded into one. In fact, as far as nourishment goes, they do seem to become a single organism. That's when they're so noticeably jellylike."

Davis watched them curiously for a few moments, and then straightened up. He moved restlessly about the room.

"The funny thing," said Gerrod cheerfully, ignoring Davis' evident gloom, "is that they seem to be able to move about.

See this test tube? They've climbed up the sides of the glass until they almost reach the top."

"I know," said Davis uninterestedly. "When we took the crew off that yacht, they showed us where the jellylike mass seemed to be slowly creeping up the sides of the ship. Looked like exaggerated capillary action."

Gerrod listened with a thoughtful frown.

"I wonder—" he began, but Davis turned to him suddenly.

"Look here, Teddy, I'm in a mess. I want your advice."

Gerrod put down his test tubes and sat on one of the tables in the laboratory, swinging his legs and preparing to be properly sympathetic with Davis' plight, which he already knew perfectly well.

"Go ahead."

"It's like this," said Davis reluctantly. "I liked Nita tremendously the first time I saw her, and she seemed to like me, too. I called on her, and she seemed to like me better. And I kept on calling. I must have pretty well infested her house, but she didn't seem to mind it, you know—"

Gerrod nodded sympathetically.

"I know."

"Well," said Davis savagely, "I found out I was pretty badly gone on her, and last week I was just getting up the nerve to propose—and I *know* she wouldn't have been displeased—when that infernal father of hers began to interfere."

"He asked you quite pleasantly," said Gerrod with a faint smile, "exactly why it was that you were coming around so often."

"And I told him," said Davis, suddenly plunged into gloom again. "It was rather premature, because I hadn't talked to Nita, but I told her father I wanted to marry her, and I loved her and all that."

"And her father," suggested Gerrod, "asked what your prospects were, and the rest of it. It takes a millionaire to be really middle class."

"That's what he did," admitted Davis miserably. "I told him my pay amounted to something, and I had about two or three thousand a year income from stocks and bonds and such things, and he laughed at me. Told me how much Nita cost him. Damn it, I don't care about how much Nita pays for dresses!"

"We men are deuced impractical," said Gerrod with a smile. "But what was her father's next move?"

"Oh"—Davis looked as if he could weep—"he was polite and all that, and said how much he liked me and such rot. Then he asked me not to see Nita again until I was in a position to offer her the things she had been raised to expect. You see the idea. He put it that he didn't want Nita to learn to care for me unless it were possible for me to make her happy and so on. It made me sick."

"I know." Gerrod nodded again. "He practically put you on honor to preserve Nita's happiness at the cost of your own."

"Damn him, yes!" Davis clenched his fists. "But Nita does care something about me. I know she does!"

Gerrod watched Davis with eyes from which he had banished every trace of a twinkle, until Davis had calmed down a little. Then he said cheerfully:

"Let's go ask Evelyn about it. His late majesty, King Solomon, once remarked that women should have the wisdom of the serpent, among other qualifications. We'll see if Evelyn comes up to Solomon's specifications."

He led the morose Davis out of the room.

The great American public became alarmed and rather resentful when its harbors were blocked by the silvery jelly. It felt, though, that the Silver Menace was more of an imposition on the part of mother nature than anything else.

Passenger traffic with Europe could be maintained by air, and freight could probably be routed through the far Northern seas to which the Silver Menace had not yet penetrated. The public considered it an annoyance, and those who were accustomed to go to the seashore lot their vacations were disgusted that the mountains would receive them that summer.

They were quite sure they did not want to go down where that slimy, disgusting, musklike odor from the stilly, silent silver sea would make their days unpleasant and the nights unendurable. Fresh fish, too, became almost prohibitive in price, as the fishing fleets were immured in the harbors that had now become mirrorlike masses of the disgusting jelly.

The public resented those things, but was not really afraid. It was not until nearly a week, after the closing of the harbors had passed that the world was informed of the Silver Menace's real threat to the human race, and began to feel little shivers of horror-stricken apprehension when it looked at the morning papers.

The news was at first passed about in swift, furtive rumors, but half believed as something too horrible to be credited. The rumors grew, however, and became more circumstantial, but the newspapers remained silent.

It is known now that the government had ordered that no hint of the new danger be allowed to become public, while its scientists worked night and day to discover a means of combating this silent, relentless threat that menaced our whole existence. Whispers flew about and became magnified, but the facts themselves could not be magnified.

At last the government could keep silence no longer, and the world was informed of the true malignity of the Silver Menace. The silvery jelly had reached the American coasts, invaded and conquered the harbors, and was even then rapidly solidifying the rivers, but its threat did not end there.

Just as it had crept up the sides of Gerrod's test tubes, and as it had overwhelmed the yacht, now it crept up the beaches. Slowly and inexorably the slimy masses of jelly crept above the water line. The beaches were buried below thick blankets of sticky, shimmering animalcules and still the menace grew.

They overwhelmed all obstacles placed in their path. The whole green, fertile earth was threatened with burial beneath a mantle of slimy, silvery, glistening horror!

CHAPTER V

Gerrod watched Davis walking hastily down to the little summerhouse, and laughed.

"Evelyn," he said, still chuckling, "you have truly the wisdom of the serpent and the gentleness of the dove. Davis falls in love with Nita. Nita's father forbids Davis the house, and then you resurrect a college friendship and invite Nita down here so their little romance can be completed. Why are women so willing to go to so much trouble for mere men?"

Evelyn slipped her arm in her husband's, and smiled up at him.

"Well-l-l," she said in mock hesitation, "perhaps this time it was because Davis is so handsome I wanted to keep out of the temptation of falling in love with him myself."

Gerrod looked after Davis. He had vanished inside the little vine-covered summerhouse, where Nita was waiting. Evelyn lifted her lips invitingly, and Gerrod responded to the invitation instantly. Both of them laughed together.

"As a husband of some six months' standing," said Gerrod with severity, "I protest against this undignified conduct you encourage me to continue."

Evelyn rubbed her cheek against his.

"We really ought to be getting back to work on those silly animals," she said reluctantly. "It's beginning to look rather serious. It may be just panic, though."

"Don't believe it." Gerrod was in earnest. "They've covered all the beaches with their sticky slime, and they're creeping inland. The rivers are choked with them, and floods are already threatening to become destructive."

"But it's so silly!" protested Evelyn. "Just because some little animalcule decides to multiply and keep on multiplying—"

"We have to get to work," finished Gerrod. "Come on into the laboratory."

They went into their workshop arm in arm. Evelyn and her husband worked together upon the problems in which they were interested, and indeed Evelyn was nearly as capable a physicist as was Gerrod. Her suggestions had helped him immensely when he and Davis battled with the cold bombs Varrhus had used in his attempt to bring the whole earth under his sway. Now they were laboring together to try to find a means of combating the silver menace that threatened the world.

"You're sure there's no exaggeration in the fear that the silver animals will actually grow up on solid ground?" asked Evelyn as she slipped into the long white apron that covered her from head to foot.

"Not much chance," said Gerrod, shaking his head. "I went down to Davis' aviation station last week. They've had to abandon the hangars nearest the water. The slimy stuff has covered the whole beach and is still creeping up. The smell is over everything, and the animals grow and grow. They've reached one of the buildings and crawled up the sides. They plastered the walls with a thick coating and even covered the roof. Height doesn't seem to bother them. They'll creep up a straight wall, and nothing seems to stop them."

"Well, they don't grow very fast," said Evelyn slowly. "There's still a lot of time left to fight them in."

"Don't believe it. They covered the Atlantic in three months. How long will they take to cover the continent?"

"You make me shiver," protested Evelyn.

"I'm doing a little shivering myself," said Gerrod grimly. "Every river in the United States is choked up with them, and they grow upstream without the least difficulty. They're creeping up the banks of the streams just as they creep over the beaches. The banks of the Hudson are a mass of silvery slime that's still expanding."

Evelyn began to look a trifle worried.

"But how far can they go from the rivers—from water?"

"They have gone three miles inland," said Gerrod grimly, "along the Carolina coast, where the shore slopes down gently to the sea. Up in Maine there are places where they have only covered a quarter of a mile. In both places, though, they are still creeping inland."

He picked up one of the test tubes.

"Something must be done to stop them. How does the cauterizing seem to work?"

"Not at all; it doesn't even make them pause."

Since their discovery that the jelly formation was caused by the tiny animalcules fusing themselves into one organism, Gerrod had thought of searing the edge of the silvery mass with a hot flame. The heat had baked and killed the animalcules for a distance of some two or three inches into the mass, and he had hoped that by that means their growth might be stopped. They had simply absorbed the seared portion into themselves as food, however, and grown on outward as before. Their means of reproduction made such a proceeding perfectly possible. Under favorable conditions of moisture and food, each of the animalcules multiplied itself by as many times as the number of tentacles it possessed. The animals themselves were tiny, jellylike creatures incased in a spherical, silicious shell from dozens of holes in which fat, restless tentacles protruded. Normally the tentacles provided the microscopic creature with the means of securing its food. Gerrod had discovered now that it was by those tentacles that they reproduced. One of the tentacles began to swell and grow a round spot at the tip. A shimmering, silvery shell appeared around the swollen portion. Within an hour from the appearance of the shimmer that showed that the protecting shell had been formed tiny, fat, jellylike tentacles protruded themselves from openings in the newly formed shell. With almost incredible rapidity the creature grew to the size of its single parent. Then the connecting tentacles snapped and a new silvery animalcule prepared to reproduce in its turn.

"And Davis is just as oblivious of the Silver Menace as if it did not exist," remarked Gerrod suddenly some time later, apropos of nothing.

Evelyn smiled indulgently and did not answer. She was trying to find if it were not possible that upon exhaustion of the food supply the animalcules would attack each other and so destroy themselves. She had sealed up small quantities of the evil-smelling jelly in test tubes where they could not possibly find fresh supplies of food. When the available nourishment was exhausted, however, they simply joined their tentacles and remained absolutely at rest, their tiny forms immobile. They did not starve, because they were using up no energy in movement. She had kept some of them for over a week in just this state of inactivity, but on being supplied with fresh water they resumed their interrupted multiplication with feverish energy.

On the beaches the slimy, silvery menace lay in absolute repose. No tremor of waves disturbed its placidity. The whole sea as far as the eye could reach was a mass of utterly quiet silver, reflecting perfectly the cloudless sky. Only at the edges of the mass was any movement visible, and that movement was a slow but inexorably sure creeping inland. Whole colonies of houses were garbed in the glistening, shining horror, and the jellylike stuff filled the roads between. And over all hung the foul, musklike odor as of slime dredged up from the bottom of the ocean.

The sun shone down perpetually from a clear blue sky now. Its fierce heat had dried out the upper surface of the silver sea into a shining mass like glistening parchment, and the breezes that blew were hot and dry. There was no longer evaporation from the sea, and the winds that blew to the shore from the ocean were like blasts from an arid desert. At night, too, the ocean no longer exerted its former function of moderator of the climate. The sun's heat was no longer absorbed by the water by day, to be given up to the breezes again at night. The winds of the ocean by day were hot, dry, foul-smelling blasts, and at night were chill and penetrating. Already the crops—which threatened to be the last ever garnered on the planet—were failing from lack of rain, and there was no relief in sight. It looked as if that part of the population which was not overwhelmed by the slimy masses of the Silver Menace would face death by starvation. Some few enterprising farmers had gone to the shore and filled wagons with the horrible jelly to spread on their farms as fertilizer. The whole world knew that the Silver Menace was simply a mass of microscopic animals, and the farmers thought they would provide their plants with animal humus by plowing the glistening stuff underground.

They soon learned their mistake. What little moisture remained in the earth was absorbed by the greedy animalcules, who multiplied exceedingly. The farmers learned of their error when they tried to cross their fields. The ground had become spongy and exuded quantities of the Silver Menace at every pore. The crops were covered with a glistening film of the horrible, sticky stuff, which weighted down and finally buried the green plants under its shining masses.

The mantle of shining horror flowed inland, always inland. It rose in thick sheets from the now solidified rivers and crept up the banks, overwhelming everything that came in its way. It clambered up tall trees, and then dripped down in long, thick ropes from their branches. Formless things, shining of silver, showed where forests had come in its way. Gangs of men were working desperately on the docks of New York, shoveling the ever-climbing masses of slimy mess back into the Hudson. Already the drains of the city were solid masses of evil-smelling liquid, and the gutters were choked with their effort to relieve the streets of the trash that was being deposited upon them. The hydrants were flushing the streets regularly now, and the fire and water departments were growing gray in their efforts to keep any fragment of silvery stuff from reaching the water-supply pipes. If that occurred the city would be helpless. As it was, the authorities were beginning to realize that they could not keep up indefinitely the fights against the ever-encroaching horror, and plans were being secretly prepared by which the entire population could be shipped away from the town when the Silver Menace could be fought off no longer.

And all this time, when the government of the greatest city in the world was recognizing the hopelessness of the city's plight and was preparing means to abandon the tall skyscrapers to the evil-smelling slime that would creep upon all the buildings and fill air the streets with glistening horror; all this time Davis and Nita spent gazing into each other's eyes, oblivious to everything but each other.

The world breathed a sigh of relief when the government announced with a fanfare of trumpets that it had found— not a way of destroying the Silver Menace, but a means of checking it. Tall board fences would be built and covered with lubricants, with greases, and other water-resisting substances. The Silver Menace would creep up to them and be helpless to clamber over them. The world would protect itself by means of dykes a thousand times more extensive than those of Holland. Men set to work frantically to build these defenses against the creeping silver flood. Five hundred miles of fencing was completed within a week, and ten thousand men increased the force of laborers day by day. Men stood behind these bulwarks and watched the slowly approaching silver tide. It crept up to the base of the oily, greasy boarding. It checked a moment.

Then it slowly and inexorably began to climb them. The lubricants were *absorbed as food by the microscopic animals, who flowed over the tall defenses and resumed their slow advance over the whole earth*!

CHAPTER VI

Davis smiled expansively and idiotically as he looked across the dinner table at Nita. Gerrod and Evelyn tried to join in his happiness, but they were both worried over the ever-increasing threat of the Silver Menace. The government's tall dykes had proven useless, and even then there were creeping sheets of the sticky slime expanding over the whole countryside. Davis and Nita, however, were utterly uninterested in such things. They gazed upon each other and smiled, and smiled. Evelyn looked at them indulgently, but Gerrod began to be faintly irritated at their absorption in each other when the world was threatened with suffocation under a blanket of slimy horror.

"It is indeed wonderful," he said with a quizzical smile, "that you two have decided to marry each other, but has it occurred to either of you that there is quite an important problem confronting the world?"

"Yes," said Davis quite seriously. "Nita's father has to be placated before we can marry."

"Please!" said Gerrod in a vexed tone. "Please stop looking at each other for one instant. I know how it feels. Evelyn and I indulge even at this late date, but for Heaven's sake think of something besides yourselves for a moment."

"Oh, you mean the silver stuff," said Nita casually. "Daddy has offered a huge reward to any one who can fight it successfully. He and half a dozen other steamship men put together and made up a purse. About two millions, I believe."

Davis was looking at her, paying but little attention to what she was saying, simply absorbed in looking. Gerrod saw his expression.

"Don't you *ever* use your head?" he demanded. "Here you are worrying about Nita's father, and there you have a reward offered that would clear away all his objections at once."

"Why—why, that's an idea!" said Davis.

"Glad you think so," said Gerrod acridly. "Suppose you two talk things over. You have a brain, Davis, even if you rarely use it."

Davis laughed good-naturedly.

After dinner Evelyn and her husband retired to the laboratory again. Neither of them wanted to waste any time that might be useful in developing a means of fighting the Silver Menace. They were deep in their work when Davis and Nita rushed in upon them.

"We've got it!" said Davis dramatically.

Nita was clinging to his arm, and looked immensely proud of him.

"What have you?" asked Gerrod practically.

"A way to clear off the Silver Menace," said Davis. "You know the animalcules have very fragile little shells. In the war we had to fight submarines with armored shells. We got the subs with depth bombs dropped near them. The concussion smashed them up. Now let's take bombs and drop them in the silver sea. The concussion will wreck the little shells for miles around."

Gerrod thought the idea, over carefully.

"It might turn the trick," he said thoughtfully.

Davis beamed.

"We'll try it at once," he said enthusiastically. "Or, rather, we'll start first thing in the morning. We must have light to experiment by. I'll phone the aviation field at once to have the big plane ready."

"I'm going, too," said Nita determinedly.

"We'll all go," said Davis expansively.

The plane left the ground shortly after daybreak. It was a curious sight to see the absolutely cloudless sunrise. The sky paled to the east, then glowed fiercely red, lightened to orange and the sun rolled up above the horizon. The big airship circled grandly until it had reached a height of nearly ten thousand feet, then swung for the east and sped away.

Nita sat in the seat beside the pilot, her face flushed with excitement. Gerrod and Evelyn occupied seats farther back, and the single engineer leaned against the rear of the car, where he could keep both ears open to the roar of his engines. The twin bomb racks along the outside of the car were filled with long, pear-shaped, high-explosive missiles, and the electric releasing switches were close beside Davis' hand. A case of hand grenades was carefully packed in the car, too.

The plane passed over green fields far below, with strangely still and shining streams and rivers winding in and out. From the banks of most of those streams glistening blankets of a silvery texture spread slowly and inexorably over the surrounding fields. Before them they saw what appeared to be the end of the world. Green fields and luxuriantly foliated forests gave place to a field of shining silver, which undulated and clumsily followed the conformation of the land and objects it had overwhelmed. Here one saw ungainly humps that seemed made of burnished metal. The rounded contours told that great trees had succumbed to the viscid mass of animalcules. There was a group of more angular forms with gaping black orifices in their glittering sides told of a village that had been abandoned to the creeping horror. The open windows of the houses yawned black and amazed, though now and then thick stalactites hung pendulously across their openings.

Above all these the big plane sped. It swept on toward the open sea—or what had been the open sea until the Silver Menace had appeared. Soon the shore was left behind, and the huge aëroplane was flying between the two skies—the real sky above and the reflected sky below. Only a thin line from far inland showed dark. All the rest seemed but a universe of air without a horizon or any sign of tangibility. Davis kept his eyes on his instruments, and presently announced:

"I think we're far enough out. We'll drop our first bomb here."

He pressed the release switch as he spoke. The plane lifted a little as the heavy bomb dropped. For a few seconds there was no sound but the roaring of the motors, but then the reverberation of the explosion below reached them.

"Take a look below," said Davis, banking the machine sharply and beginning to swing in a narrow circle.

Gerrod looked down. He saw what seemed to be a ring of yellowish smoke, and a dark-blue spot in the middle of the silvery mass beneath them.

"It did something," he reported, "There's a dark spot on the surface. I can't judge how large it is, though."

Davis released a second bomb, and a third. Gerrod could watch them as they fell. They dwindled from winged, pear-shaped objects to dots. Then there was a flash far below and a spurting of water and spray. In a moment that had subsided, and he saw a second and larger dark-blue spot beside the first.

"I believe you've done it," said Gerrod excitedly. "You've certainly destroyed the silvery appearance. Dare you go lower?"

"Surely," said Davis cheerfully. The plane dived like an arrow, and flattened out barely five hundred feet above the surface.

Gerrod examined the dark spots through glasses. The disturbance had not completely abated, and he could see indubitable waves still radiating from the Spot where the bombs had fallen. Davis grinned like a boy when Gerrod told him.

"We'll land in the open space and make sure," he said suddenly, and the plane dived again.

Before Gerrod could protest they were just skimming the surface of the silver sea. The plane settled gently into the now liquid spot of ocean, and Davis shut off the motors. The occupants of the cabin looked eagerly out of the windows. All about them, in a space perhaps sixty or seventy yards across, the water was yellowed and oily, but was certainly water, and not the horrible, jellylike stuff the world had so much cause to fear. The concussion from the high-explosive bomb had shattered the fragile shells of the silver animalcules, and, with their protection gone, they had relapsed into liquid. At the edge of that space, however, the silver-sea began again, as placid and malignant as before.

The plane floated lightly on the surface while the little party congratulated itself.

"It works," said Davis proudly. Nita squeezed his hand ecstatically.

"I knew he'd think of something," she announced cheerfully.

Evelyn and Gerrod were estimating the area of cleared water with gradually lengthening faces.

"Let's see how much space a hand grenade clears," suggested Evelyn thoughtfully.

Davis opened the case and took out one of the wicked little bombs. He wriggled through a window and out on the massive lower plane of the flying boat. Balancing himself carefully, he flung the grenade some sixty yards into the untouched silver sea. It burst with a cracking detonation and amid a fountain of spume and spray. The four of them eyed the resultant area of clear water.

"How wide do you suppose that is?" asked Gerrod rather depressedly.

"Ten—no, fifteen yards by fifteen."

So excited were they all that they did not notice a phenomenon that began almost instantly. The tiny animalcules that formed the silver sea reproduced rapidly when given merely moisture. Here they had that moisture, and, in addition, the bodies of all their dead comrades to feed upon. The conditions were ideal for nearly instantaneous reproduction. As a result the waves from the high-explosive bombs had hardly subsided when the open space began, almost imperceptibly, to be closed by fresh masses of the Silver Menace. The open space became covered with a thin film which became thicker—thicker—

"And how much explosive was in that grenade?"

"Two ounces of TNT." Davis began to catch the drift of the questions, and his happy expression was beginning to fade away.

"Two ounces of TNT cleared up roughly a hundred and fifty square yards of silver sea. That's, say, seventy-five square yards to the ounce of high explosive." Evelyn was working rapidly with her pencil. "That works out—five hundred pounds of TNT needed to clear a square mile of the Silver Menace. We have fifteen hundred miles of coast that has been invaded to an average depth of at least five miles."

Gerrod took up the calculations with a dismal face. His pencil moved quickly for a moment or so.

"We'd need over eighteen hundred tons of TNT to clear our coasts," he said dolefully. "That wouldn't touch the silver sea itself or keep it from growing again. It grew inland those five miles in two weeks at most. That's nine hundred tons a week needed to hold our own without attacking the silver sea at all. We'd have to have forty-six thousand tons a year to *hold* it, let alone go after the beasts out here, and in the meantime we'll have no rain, consequently no crops. It's a cheerful outlook."

They had been oblivious of what was happening immediately about the seaplane.

Nita first saw the danger.

"Look!" she gasped.

They had been too much absorbed in gloomy thoughts to notice their predicament. The open space in which they had landed was now a shining, glittering mass of the Silver Menace. But what Nita pointed to was of more imminent danger. The sticky, horrible mass was creeping up the float on which the seaplane rode and up the smaller floats at the ends of the wings. Tons of the silver horror had already accumulated upon the under surface of the great planes and weighted down the aëroplane until it was impossible for it to rise in the air. And it continued to creep up and over the body. In a little while the seaplane would be overwhelmed by the viscid, evil-smelling, deadly little animalcules.

CHAPTER VII

Shining slime crawled up the small floats at the ends of the lower wing. It crept along the under surface, and then dripped in thick ropes down to the surface below. When contact was established the ropes grew fat and wider, until they were like shining columns from the silver sea to the now heavily weighted plane. The disgusting stuff crept over the edges of the lower plane, and began to spread over its upper surface. Other masses began to creep up the struts that separated the lower plane from the top.

The three men began to work like mad. They tore strips from the roof of the cabin and began feverishly to scrape off and thrust away the insistently advancing enemy. The plane was a large one, however, and no sooner had they scraped clear one portion of the plane than another portion was covered even more thickly than the first. The cabin itself began to be attacked. Its lower portion already glistened like metal, and in a little while the silvery film began to cover the glass of the windows. Nita began to be frightened. Parts of the roof had been torn away to provide the three men—Davis, Gerrod, and the engineer—with the means of fighting the creeping horror. When the slime reached the roof and began, to pour down the opening there, the whole cabin would become a terrible, suffocating tank of the horrible stuff. Evelyn spoke quietly, though with a white face.

"If you start the motors the wind from the propellers may blow the jelly away from the cabin."

The engineer leaped to one of the propellers and swung his weight upon it. The engine turned sluggishly, and then coughed. A second desperate heave. The motor began to run with a roar. The surface of the slime on which the blast of wind beat shivered, and then reluctantly began to retreat. The second motor burst into bellowing activity. The whole plane began to shiver and tremble from the efforts of the powerful engines to draw it forward, but the jelly in which it was gripped still held it fast. The three men redoubled their efforts, and now some faint result began to show. Hampered by the vibrations which strove to shake it off, the Silver Menace advanced less rapidly. In half an hour the upper surface of the plane was nearly free. There was nearly a solid wall of silver horror connecting its under portion with the jellied ocean below.

Davis came to the cabin window, wiping the sweat from his forehead.

"There's only one chance," he shouted above the roar of the engines. "I've got to fling hand grenades into the sea just ahead of us. They may clear a way for us to rise."

Nita silently began to pass him up the small but deadly missiles. Her face was set and utterly pale, but she was rising to the emergency with spirit.

An explosion sounded fifty yards away. Another thirty yards away. A third but twenty yards away, and the plane heaved and leaped from the concussion. The blast of air nearly blew the three men from the wings into the waiting mass of animalcules. A huge volume of ill-smelling spume was cast upon the plane, and by its velocity washed away a great portion of the Silver Menace that still clung to it. The propellers dragged at the plane, and it suddenly darted forward down the narrow lane of open water cleared by the three explosions. All three of the men were clinging to struts out on the plane and there was no one at the controls, but Nita bravely grasped the joy stick, and as the end of the open water drew rapidly near she jerked it backward with an inward prayer. The plane lifted sluggishly, scraped the top of the silver sea, and rose. With an inexperienced pilot at the wheel, with the three men precariously balanced on the wings, it headed straight for the broadest part of the Atlantic.

The motors roared as the plane continued to rise. Nita was white-faced and frightened, but Davis' life was depending upon her. With an amazing coolness, despite the lump in her throat that threatened to choke her, she swung the steering wheel as she had seen Davis do. The plane turned in a wide half circle and headed for the shore again, still rising. Davis, out on the wing, took a desperate chance. He motioned wildly to Evelyn, who flung wide the side window. Then, diving as in a football game, Davis flung himself for the opening. His hands caught in the frame and he drew himself inside. As he laid his hands on the controls Nita incontinently fainted, but Evelyn was there to attend to her, and Davis sped for home at the topmost speed of which the plane was capable, the other two men still clinging to the struts far out on the wings.

Alexander Morrison, steamship magnate and many times a millionaire, looked helplessly from the window of his library. His daughter, Nita, was visiting Evelyn Gerrod, a college classmate, and there was no one to sympathise with him in his misfortune. He faced absolute ruin. The whole world faced death, but that did not impress Morrison as much as the absolute financial disaster that had come upon him. His ships, at their docks, were useless and already incrusted with the silvery slime that threatened the whole earth. His whole fortune was invested in those vessels. When the government had thrown up its hands over the problem of checking the invasion of the Silver Menace, far less of clearing the seas again, Morrison had gone hopelessly to his little country home on one of the infrequent islands of the Hudson. It was a high and rocky little island, and his house was built upon the top of its single peak. He could look out upon the now solid Hudson and see miles and miles of the silver, evil-smelling jelly.

A little bridge connected the island with the mainland, to which a well-made, winding road led down. Morrison stared through his closed library window—closed to keep out the slimy, disgusting odor of the Silver Menace—and cursed the microscopic animals that had ruined all commerce and now threatened to destroy humanity. Of all his great fleet but two of the smallest vessels remained afloat. They were high up in northern seas, still unvisited by the jellylike animalcules. Where his tramp steamers and passenger lines had visited nearly every port upon the globe, now two small ships plied between Greenland and the most northern part of the American continent.

The silvery jelly was clambering up the rocky shores of his little island, but beyond cursing it Morrison paid no attention. He was absorbed in his misfortune, utterly preoccupied with the calamity that had overwhelmed him. For two days he moved restlessly about his house, smoking innumerable cigars, eating hardly anything, thinking of nothing but the extent of the disaster to his fortune. He had offered half a million dollars to whoever developed a successful means of combating the Silver Menace. Other men whose wealth, like his own, was solely invested in ocean transportation had joined him in offering rewards, until now a purse of two and a half millions awaited the successful inventor. Multitudes of freak proposals had been made, the majority of them suggesting that sea gulls be trained to eat the silver animalcules, or that fish be bred in large numbers to consume them. In practice, of course, neither fish or birds would touch the disgusting jelly. The arctic seas were teeming with practically all the fish from the Atlantic Ocean. For once the Eskimos had no difficulty in securing enough to eat. The inhabitants of the seas in which the Silver Menace had appeared, without exception, fled from its sticky masses.

Morrison remained shut up in his house, sunk in despondency and gloom, while the silvery jelly crept up the shores of his little island slowly but surely, higher and higher day by day. His butler came to him with a white face.

"Mr. Morrison, sir," said the butler hesitatingly, "the gardener says, sir, that that there silver stuff is creepin' up higher, sir."

"All right, let it creep!" snapped Morrison angrily.

"But, sir," ventured the butler once more, "it's creepin' up on the bridge."

"Have it shoveled down again," said Morrison irritably. "Don't bother me."

The butler went out of the room, and ten minutes later the two gardeners went down to the bridge with shovels. They scraped and shoveled industriously, and when darkness fell the bridge was clear. But next morning showed the bridge a mass of shining silver, and not only the bridge, but fifty or a hundred yards of the roadway and turf leading up to it. The animalcules had come upon the green grass and it had been used for food, so that they were multiplying rapidly. The creeping movement of the silvery tide could be distinctly seen. The butler came to Morrison in a panic.

"Oh, Mr. Morrison, sir," he said tremulously, "the bridge is covered again and the horrible stuff is coming up to the house. You can see it move, sir. We'll all be suffocated when it catches us, sir."

Morrison shook his head impatiently.

"Don't bother me."

The butler was trembling fitfully, "Beg pardon, sir, but the men says as they won't stay no longer, and they're going to try to get over the bridge to the mainland, sir."

"Very well, let them."

The butler left the room. Presently Morrison heard an uproar outside. The butler was protesting at the top of his voice against something. Morrison went out to see what was the matter. Even his indifference was penetrated by the sight he saw. The silvery slime had crept up to a point but a hundred yards from the house, and was still slowly advancing. Half a dozen servants were bringing out one of Morrison's cars, and were evidently planning to make a dash in it, despite the efforts of the butler to hold them back. Morrison stepped forward.

"Wait a moment, James," he said quietly. "Let the men have the car, but it would be better for one to make the attempt first. There's no use all risking their lives until we know whether there's a chance of success."

His chauffeur was hastily tuning up a motor cycle.

"I'll make a try, sir," he said grimly. "I'll circle the house once or twice until I get up speed, and then shoot for the bridge. I think I'll make it."

Morrison nodded. The motor cycle caught and began to run. The chauffeur circled the lawn once—twice. His machine was running at a terrific speed. He came around the third time, swung on the handlebars, and shot straight for the bridge. The silvery slime shot away from his front wheels in twin waves as he cut through the mass. The throttle was wide open and the engine worked manfully. Straight for the bridge he went, plowing through the thick, sticky mass. Then the accumulated volume of jelly before him broke down the impetus of his cycle. In spite of all he could do it slowed down, down. It tottered weakly and fell. The chauffeur leaped from it and plunged forward. He slipped and fell, then struggled to his feet again. Five feet more, ten feet more. He was like an animated statue of burnished metal. Thick ropes of silver clung to him as he struggled forward. No man could keep up such exertions. He labored with almost insane force, but his progress became slower and slower. At last he moved forward no more, but still straggled weakly. Then he toppled gently from his feet. The slime covered him silently and placidly. The watchers gasped. The silver tide grew slowly toward the house.

CHAPTER VIII

Nita was clinging to Davis' hand as they drove out to the Gerrods' cottage again. Traces of her fright still lingered on her face, and Davis' hand was comforting. Gerrod and Evelyn were silent and discouraged. The only really promising plan for fighting the Silver Menace had proven so ineffectual as to be practically useless. In silence the little motor car wound along the twisting road to the little cottage.

All of them were quiet, even gloomy, as they sat down to lunch. Evelyn tried to talk lightly, but conversation lagged in spite of her efforts. The maid brought in their dishes and removed others without a sound. None of them could eat more than a very little.

When the meal was finished Gerrod and Evelyn went out on the porch to discuss gravely the chances, even now, of producing the explosive needed to hold back the Silver Menace. The almost instantaneous reproduction that had taken place over the cleared area at sea, however, made it evident that nine hundred tons of explosive would be needed, not every week, but every day. All the factories in the country, working at their highest speed, could not supply the quantity necessary.

Davis went into the laboratory and brought out one of the silvery test tubes of animalcules.

"Nita," he said mournfully, "I've fought Germans and come out on top. Gerrod and I fought Varrhus and won out. But these infernal little animals, so small I have to take a microscope to see them, seem to have me beaten."

Nita's soft hand crept up and snuggled inside Davis' larger one.

"No, they haven't, either," she insisted stoutly. "You'll think of something yet."

Davis sighed.

"And it would be so perfect if we could be the ones to find out how to beat them," he said dolefully. "That would satisfy your father, and we'd have nothing else to worry about."

Nita looked up into his solemn face, and, in spite of herself, laughed.

"You're worrying too much," she announced. "We're going to take a vacation and go into the music room and I'm going to play soft music that will take your mind off your troubles."

She led him into the tiny music room of the bungalow, and sat down at the small grand piano there.

"You can turn over the music for me," she said gravely as she made room for him on the seat before the keyboard.

There was no music on the rack of the piano, but neither of them thought of that. Davis set down the test tube he had brought with him and prepared to listen. Nita quite forgot to play any recognizable melody, too. Davis thoughtlessly took possession of her left hand, so she idly struck chords with her right, while the two of them talked foolishnesses that were very delightful. They spoke in low tones, and their voices were soft. They were having an amazingly pleasant time.

They heard footsteps on the porch, and self-consciously drew apart. Gerrod and Evelyn were coming indoors to go back into the laboratory to work on wearily in hopes of stumbling on something that might have an effect upon the ever-encroaching Silver Menace. Davis hastily picked up the test tube full of animalcules. As he took it in his hands, however, he uttered an exclamation of astonishment. The contents were no longer silvery! The tube was full of water with a faintly yellowish tinge. Davis' jaw dropped.

"People!" he called hastily. "Come here! Something has happened!"

Gerrod and Evelyn appeared in the doorway.

"What's the matter?"

"Something's happened to these little beasts." Davis held out the test tube. "Twenty minutes ago this was full of the silver stuff. I put it down on the sounding board here and now they're smashed up and dead!"

Gerrod looked at the tube intently.

"Where was it?"

Davis showed him. Gerrod put one hand on the spot and struck a chord tentatively. His expression changed from weariness to hope.

"Wait a minute!" he exclaimed, and darted into the laboratory, to return a moment later with half a dozen test tubes full of the sticky animalcules. "We'll put another one there and strike a chord."

He did so. The contents of the test tube remained unchanged. He struck another. Still no change. Then, deliberately striking one key after the other, with the eyes of all four of them fixed hopefully on the test tube, he began to go up the keyboard. Note after note was struck, but just as they were about to give up hopes of finding the cause of the first tube's clearing Gerrod struck a key—the *F* above high *C*. The instant the shrill note sounded out the test tube clouded—and was clear! It had lain upon the sounding board of the piano. The vibrations of the piano string had been communicated to it through the sounding board.

"*Done!*" shouted Davis at the top of his voice.

Nita was speechless.

"Sympathetic vibrations," said Gerrod happily. "If you could hang up one of those microscopic shells and ring it it would ring that note. So, when the vibrations from the piano strike them, they vibrate in sympathy, only the piano vibrations are so strong and the shells so fragile that they rack themselves to bits, and the animals are killed. Whee! Hurray! Hurray!"

He shook hands all around, hardly, able to contain his excitement.

"But I say," said Davis anxiously, "will those vibrations travel through water, and can we put a piano overboard?"

Gerrod laughed.

"We'll put a submarine siren overboard," he said excitedly, "and tune it to that note. You can hear a submarine siren for fifteen miles with an under-water telephone. Man, you've done the trick!"

The maid appeared in the doorway.

"Some one on the telephone for Miss Morrison."

Nita reluctantly left the room where the others were chattering excitedly. She went to the telephone and put the receiver to her ear, still unconsciously trying to catch the words of the party in the music room. Almost the first words she heard drove them from her mind, however. Her father was speaking.

"Nita," he was saying coolly, "this is your father. I'm marooned in the house on the island, and the Silver Menace is climbing up the walls. The windows are blocked. I'm expecting them to break in any minute. When they do I'm done."

"Daddy!" Nita choked, aghast.

"Simmons, the chauffeur, tried to get across the bridge this morning," said her father still more coolly, "and the sticky stuff got him. The room I'm in is dark. The Silver Menace has climbed up to the roof. We've stopped up the chimney so it can't come down to get us, but when the house is completely covered we'll be in an air-tight case that will suffocate us sooner or later. I'm rather hoping the windows will break in before that time. I'd rather die like Simmons this morning."

"But, daddy, daddy, hold on! We'll come to you—"

"It can't be done," her father interrupted crisply. "I called you to say good-by and to tell you to look after the families of the servants that are fastened up here with me." He paused a moment, and said quietly: "I'm in the library downstairs. I can hear the windows creaking. They may give way at any moment and let the horror into the house. It tried to creep in under the doorsills, but we calked them with the table linen."

"Daddy!" cried Nita agonizedly. "Oh, daddy, try to fight it off just a little while! We've found a way to stop it! We can kill them all!"

"I have about ten minutes more, Nita," said her father gently. "You couldn't get to me. Be a good girl, Nita—" There was a crash. "There go the windows! Good-by, Nita, good-by—"

The others heard her cry out, and rushed from the music room to hear her calling, calling desperately for her father to answer her, calling into a silent phone.

CHAPTER IX

Davis pounded mightily upon the great gate of the half-deserted shipyard. Behind him, Nita was sobbing in spite of her efforts to hold back her tears. Evelyn tried her best to calm Nita, but without real effect. Gerrod had shot the party out at the gate of the shipyard and darted off in the little motor car on some mysterious errand. Davis pounded again wrathfully, using a huge stone to make his blows reverberate through the yard. A workman came slowly toward them.

"Hurry! Hurry!" Nita called tearfully. "Please hurry!"

The workman recognized her through the palings. All of Morrison's employees knew his daughter. The workman broke into a run. The gate swung open.

"Where's Mr. Keeling, the manager?" demanded Nita urgently. "We must see him at once."

The workman pointed, and the three of them hurried as fast as they could walk toward the man he had indicated.

"Mr. Keeling," said Nita desperately. "Father is marooned in our house up the Hudson. He may be dead by now. We've got to get to him!"

"I don't know how—" began the manager helplessly.

"I want a submarine siren," said Davis crisply. "One that can be tuned to different notes. Also the fastest motor boat you have. Give the necessary orders at once."

"But the Silver Menace—" began the manager again.

"Don't stand there talking," barked Davis in a tone that secured instant obedience. "Get the siren and the boat. And hurry! This is life and death!"

Galvanized into action, but still confused, the manager gave the orders. A fast motor boat that had been hauled ashore and pot into a shed when the Silver Menace blocked the river was hauled out. A heavy submarine siren was hastily unearthed from one of the workshops, and Davis drove the workmen to the task of fitting a sling on the boat by which the siren could be lowered over the bow. A heavy crane was run up and the motor boat made fast, in readiness to be lifted overboard. Every one worked with the utmost speed of which they were capable. Davis was not his usual good-natured self now. He drove his workmen mercilessly. Hardly had the last of their preparations been completed when a heavy truck rumbled into the yard. Gerrod had commandeered the truck and worked wonders. A grand piano had been lifted bodily into the big automobile. As the truck stopped he was lifting the lid that protected the keys. An electrician stood by the siren, with the tuning apparatus exposed. Hardly had the engine of the truck been shut off when they were busy tuning the blast of the siren to match the tinkling sound of the piano. It took a heart-breakingly long time to get the pitches precisely alike, but then the launch swung high in the air and alighted on the surface of the jelly below. The electrician in the launch pressed the button that would set the siren at work sending out its blast of sound waves through the water.

Those on the bank watched in agonized apprehension. The siren sank into the jelly like mass. No audible sound issued from it, once it was submerged, but when the curious sound waves issued into the water from the giant metal plate that in normal times carried warnings to ships at sea a change was visible in the jelly. Where ever the curious water sound traveled the silvery jelly clouded and abruptly turned to liquid! Almost instantly the space between the two wharves, in which the launch lay, was free of the horrible stuff. Gerrod shouted excitedly. Davis swore happily. Nita pushed anxiously forward.

"We've got to get to daddy!" she cried desperately. "We mustn't waste a second! Not an instant!"

The four of them piled into the launch. An engineer leaped down and twisted the motor. The fast launch shot forward, the submarine siren at the bow sending out its strange water sound that was inaudible to those on board, but which had such an amazing effect on the microscopic animals that composed the silver sea. As the launch gathered speed and headed up the Hudson a high bow wave spread out on either side. The water on which they rode was yellowed and malodorous, but it was water, and not the silvery, slime that had threatened the world. The Silver Menace vanished before the launch as if by magic. When the motor boat approached, with its siren still sounding fiercely, though inaudibly, the jellied surface of the river shivered into yellowed liquid, and the creeping horror on the banks trembled and became a torrent of water that flowed eagerly back into the bed of the stream.

The island on which Morrison had been marooned loomed up ahead, looking like a small mountain of silver. The house at its top was as a monument of shining metal. But as the boat sped toward it the silvery appearance of the coating clouded and melted away. Instead a torrent of evil-smelling water poured down the sloping sides of the island and into the river again!

They found the servants weeping for joy. Morrison, when the windows of the library had broken in under the weight of the mass of the horror outside, had leaped through the door of the library and slammed the door behind him. They had calked the cracks with cloth, and for a moment isolated the Silver Menace in that one room. As window after window broke in, however, they had been forced to withdraw from room to room, until at last they were huddled together in a tiny linen closet, windowless and without ventilation. They were waiting there for death when they heard the rushing of water all about them and found the Silver Menace, silver and a menace no longer, flowing down to rejoin the waters from which it had come.

As is the way of women, Nita, having sobbed heartbrokenly for sorrow when she believed her father dead, now sobbed even more heartbrokenly for joy at finding him alive, but she did not neglect, after a reasonable interval, to bring Davis forward.

"You know him, daddy," she said, smiling. "Well, he is the person who found the way to destroy the Silver Menace, and so he's the person you are going to pay that big reward to."

Morrison shook hands with Davis. He knew what was coming next.

"And though it hasn't anything to do with the other things," Nita said proudly, "he's the person I'm going to marry."

"It would be ungracious," observed Morrison, "to disagree with you. Mr. Davis, you are a lucky man."

"I know it," said Davis, laughing in some embarrassment. He looked at Nita, who dimpled at him, and was promptly and frankly kissed for her daring. She did not seem to mind, however. In fact, she dimpled again.

The last vestige of the Silver Menace was turned to yellowed water within a month. Submarine sirens, carefully tuned to precisely the pitch that would cause the tiny shells to shatter themselves, were hastily set aboard huge numbers of fast steamers, that swept the ocean in patrols, clearing the sea as they went. Whenever the clear note was poured out by one of the under-water sirens the silvery animalcules died in their myriads. Slowly, as the evil smell of their bodies dissipated, the inhabitants of the Atlantic Ocean came back to their normal haunts. By shoals and schools, by swarms and in tribes, the fishes came down again from the North. A week after the destroying steamers began their patrol rain fell on the Atlantic coast. The abnormally dry air above the ocean took up water avidly and poured it down on the parched earth with a free hand. The ocean, too, took up again its former function of furnishing cool breezes during the day and warm breezes at night. The seashore became once more a place of charm and delight. At least Davis and Nita found it so. Davis was being waited upon with decorations and honorary degrees, with the freedom of cities and medals of honor from learned societies. At each presentation solemn speeches were made in which he was told how superlatively clever he was. Remembering the purely accidental nature of his discovery, he found it difficult to keep from laughing. These things were tiresome, but were not active nuisances until after his marriage. When he found that he and Nita would not be left alone, that no matter how scrupulously they concealed their identity it was sooner or later discovered and they were interviewed and written up in special articles for the newspapers he grew annoyed.

The climax came on a beautifully moonlit night at a seashore resort where they were quite confident they would not be discovered. The beach was like silver, and the waves were dark and mysterious, except where the reflection of the moon glittered on their shining sides. Davis and Nita, forgetting the world and devoutly hoping that they were by the world forgot, sat and looked at the moon and played idly in the sand and told each other the eternal foolishnesses that are probably the truest wisdom. They were utterly happy just being alone with each other.

A dark figure looked up over and coughed. They started.

"You are Flight Commander and Mrs. Davis?" said a voice deprecatingly.

Davis groaned and admitted it.

"Our little villagers learned that you are visiting here, and a banquet has been prepared in the pavilion in your honor. Won't you do us the honor to attend?"

Davis muttered several words under his breath, for which Nita later reprimanded him, and rose heavily.

The banquet was a great success. The freedom of the village was given them both. Speeches were made, in which

Davis was told how superlatively clever he was. The band played "See the Conquering Hero Comes." Davis sat miserably through it all, with Nita, scarcely less miserable, by his side.

The next morning he sent a wire to Teddy Gerrod:

> Can we come and spend our honeymoon with you? People won't let us alone.
>
> Davis.

Within an hour the answer came:

> Come along. We'll let you alone. We're having a second honeymoon ourselves.
>
> Gerrod.

Davis showed the wire to Nita.

"Splendid!" she said with a sigh of relief. Then she dimpled and looked up at Davis. "But, Dicky, dear, we'll never have a second honeymoon like they are having."

"We won't?" demanded Davis. "Why not?"

"Because," said Nita, putting her face very close to his. "Because our first one is never going to stop."